The Baker's

Christmas

Miracle

Mail Order Brides of Dayton Falls

(Book Five)

Copyright

Dedication

To Margaret Tanner, my very dear friend and fellow author, for her enduring encouragement and friendship.

To Alan, my husband of over forty-eight years, who has been a relentless supporter of my writing and dreams for many years.

To You, my wonderful readers, who encourage me to continue writing these stories. It is such a joy knowing so many of you enjoy reading my stories as much as I love writing them for you.

Table of Contents

Chapter One

Westlake, Wyoming – 1880

Abigail Martin leaned against the flour-covered counter and sighed.

The bakery was busy today, busier than she'd anticipated. There was a lot of work to be done before she could leave for the day.

"Abigail!" Her father was not pleased. He'd obviously noticed her standing around doing nothing. She felt sorry for him as he worked far longer hours than she did.

He was up with the birds to get the ovens fired up and prepared for baking. "Yes, Father," she said meekly, knowing it was senseless to argue. He always won.

He'd been good to her over the years, reared her after Mother had suddenly died when she was a small child, but now she was a slave to his whims.

She worked from dawn until dusk for nothing more than board and lodgings.

Abigail glanced around – one day this would all be hers. With no older brother to snatch it from under her, it was something to look forward to, even if it was some years away.

Abigail scrubbed at the counter, ensuring it was spotless. Next she'd tackle the tables. Now that all the customers had left, it was easier to clean up.

She rinsed the kitchen cloth in the warm soapy water and moved onto the first table. Peter Jones and his rowdy friends had sat there last. They'd spilled food all over the tabletop, no doubt on purpose to cause her more work.

Peter had asked her six times now to marry him, and she'd refused him every time. She knew the likes of him. He'd never once had a nice word to say to her. Treated her like a slave, not a potential wife.

No, his eyes were on the bakery, not the baker's daughter.

When she met the man she was destined to marry, she'd know. And until then, she wouldn't set off down the wedding aisle. She certainly wouldn't be doing it for the likes of him. He was nothing but a gold digger.

When she finished cleaning the tables, she tackled the chairs. She scrubbed them all down every night, then swept the floor.

Last thing before she left at night, she scrubbed the floors until they shone. She didn't mind the hard work, not really, but it would be nice to get something for her trouble. Even a few measly dollars would be acceptable.

She had to rely on her father for everything, even down to her cheap gowns and work aprons.

"Abigail," he yelled as he finished cleaning the last oven. She hurried over to see what her father wanted.

She looked into his face. He looked far more tired recently, and she wondered if he might be unwell.

"Yes, Father?"

He slammed the oven door shut and stared at her. "We need to talk." He led her over to the recently scrubbed tables and sat, indicating she should do the same.

When he stared at her for over a minute, she began to worry. "You're scaring me, Father," she said quietly. Was he ill and dying? She couldn't bear it if he was.

He reached across the table for her hand. "I've decided to sell the bakery," he said gruffly.

She stared at him in horror. "Sell the bakery?" Her inheritance? She'd worked so hard for many years with nothing to show for it. And now this.

Surely he would give her some of the funds from the sale? The moment the thought entered her head she knew it would never happen.

She swallowed hard. "When is this to occur?"

He smiled. Surely he didn't think she was happy with his decision?

"I'll hand it over in six weeks. In the meantime, we are to teach Mr Jones everything there is to know about running a bakery."

Mr Jones? Surely not…

"I also promised Peter that you would become his wife. It's in the contract." He leaned back and crossed his arms across his chest. "You won't let me down, will you, Abigail?"

He glared at her, as though he was daring her to refuse. "No, Father," she said, all the while her mind was ticking over trying to fathom how she could get out of this disastrous contract her father had negotiated without her permission.

"Good." He pushed back his chair and stood. "Mr Jones will be here at the crack of dawn Monday, expecting to begin learning the trade."

Abigail's hands were fisted at her sides. How dare her father make such an outrageous deal with a man she despised. And how dare he include her as part of the sale!

She determined then and there not to be sold like a side of beef. If Mr Peter Jones thought she would go quietly, he had another think coming.

* * *

"My dear girl," Miss Bethany Wilde of the Mail Order Bride Agency told her. "There are several young men looking for brides right now." She shuffled some papers around her desk, until she finally settled on a small pile of hand written sheets.

"I don't care who or where it is as long as it's not here in Wyoming." Abigail was adamant. If she was too close to home, Peter Jones was likely to drag her back kicking and screaming, forcing her to marry him.

Miss Bethany, as she preferred to be called, shuffled through the papers. "That eliminates several of these potential grooms then." She pulled out the offending pages and put them aside.

Abigail reached out and snatched one of the remaining pages from her hands. "This one will do." It was obvious from her expression Miss Bethany was horrified she'd made the decision without even reading the information provided.

"Oh no, Miss Martin. That won't do – you must select a groom. I pride myself on matching…"

She was interrupted by Abigail's words. "Matching? There is no matching when it's all by mail, surely?"

Miss Bethany stared at her open-mouthed, but Abigail was having none of it. "I must leave immediately. My father has sold me to a man, along with his business."

There, she'd said it. It sounded just as vulgar now as it did when her father had first said the words to her.

"Oh my dear girl…" Miss Bethany was visibly upset at this information. "When do you plan to leave?"

Abigail took a deep breath. "Immediately. He's taking over the business Monday."

Miss Bethany flew into action, and provided Abigail with all the relevant information. "You will love Dayton Falls," she said. "I've sent several brides there now, and they've all settled in very well and eventually fallen in love with their husbands."

Abigail swallowed. She didn't care much for love right now. What was more important was getting as far away from Wyoming as she could in the shortest possible time. The quicker she married, the more unavailable she was to Peter Jones.

* * *

Dayton Falls, Montana

Ethan Harper looked up from his position on the floor where he was assembling the display cases.

He glanced over to where his brother Patrick, a carpenter, was working and was surprised to see people huddled around, watching his every move.

He knew when he'd purchased this empty store it would garner some interest, but he didn't realize how much.

His plan had been to move in quietly and prepare the store for opening day without an audience. It was now obvious that wasn't going to happen.

He dropped the hammer to the floor and stood up, stretching the muscles that had begun to cramp. How long had he been down there?

Checking his pocket-watch, Ethan discovered it was well over two hours. Time for a break anyway.

He brushed the sawdust off himself and ran his fingers through his chestnut colored hair. He stood staring at the group of women standing outside in the cold morning air, then strolled outside to join them.

"Good morning, ladies," he said amiably. "How can I help you?"

They all began talking at once – it was like a gabble of turkeys.

He held up a dusty hand. "One at a time, please!" They all looked at one woman, an older lady, who stepped forward.

"Good morning to you, Sir," she said. "Allow me to introduce myself. I am Mrs Jensen. We were wondering what you are building here? Is it something of interest to the wives of Dayton Falls?"

He smiled. He couldn't help himself. His humble little store had drawn some interest, and it wasn't even open yet.

"Well ladies," he said slowly. "I rather think it might." He took his time and drew out the next words. "Very soon we'll be done here, and the bakery will open."

"Ooooh, a bakery!"

"Wonderful."

"Finally."

Several of the women all spoke at once - it warmed his heart to think the store wasn't even open yet, but there was sufficient interest to almost guarantee his business would be successful.

He held his hand up again. The gabble was beginning to get to him.

Mrs Jensen stepped closer. "May we know when you are opening?"

"In two weeks," he said, and watched as her eyes took in the mess that was his new bakery. "It looks like a mess now, but trust me, it will be ready in time."

He hoped and prayed that was true. The next train into Dayton Falls was bringing his ovens and the crew to install them, plus the rest of his equipment.

"Oh, and ladies," he said, a huge grin on his face. "It will also be a café – a place for you wonderful ladies to sit and have a coffee and a chat."

The women began to chat between themselves, then Mrs Jensen stepped forward and spoke again. "What of your wife," she asked. "When is she arriving?"

He stared at the woman. Why did everyone automatically assume he had a wife? "I, I'm not married," he finally answered. A wife was the last thing he wanted. Or needed.

They collectively stopped and stared at him. "Perhaps it's something you should seriously consider," Mrs Jensen told him sternly. "She could be an enormous help with running your business." The others followed when she spun around and stormed off, leaving him to stare after them and wonder if Mrs Jensen could be right.

Chapter Two

Abigail stared out the window of the monstrosity she was forced to endure.

The soot and dirt covered her face, and no matter how many times she cleaned it off, it was almost instantaneously back again.

She flicked at the soot on her gown – she was nearly at her destination and she would arrive a mess. Not that she wasn't used to mess, she was regularly covered in flour, but that was different. It was at least for a purpose.

The soot – it was horrid stuff.

"Next stop, Dayton Falls." The conductor walked along the narrow aisles informing the passengers of the next destination.

Her heart rate hitched. She couldn't believe she'd snatched a letter out of Miss Bethany's hands and decided that would be her destiny.

She knew nothing of this man – this... She pulled the note out of her pocket and stared at it. Ethan Harper.

Abigail wondered what he would be like. She didn't even know how old he was. Then she remember the envelope she'd been given as she left the mail order bride agency.

Suddenly curious, she opened it. Her eyes scanned the beautiful copperplate handwriting.

Ethan Harper – her betrothed – was a baker. She groaned out loud. That was the last thing she needed. Going from one bakery to another.

She understood now why Miss Bethany wanted her to read the letter before deciding.

Well, it was too late now. At least he didn't know anything about her, and that's the way it would stay.

"Dayton Falls. Dayton Falls." The conductor shouted as he strolled along the aisles. Abigail would not leave her seat until the contraption stopped. She recalled a trip as a young child where she stood too early, and found herself sprawled out on the floor from the sudden jerking as the train came to a halt.

The moment it stopped completely she stood and reached for her carpetbag. Not that it contained much. She owned little, but she had to get away as quickly as possible, and didn't dare pack her bag while Father was awake.

Had she been caught, she would be little more than a prisoner. He was determined to marry her off to the obnoxious Peter Jones, and that just wouldn't do.

The conductor stood at the bottom of the steps and reached out for her hand, helping her down. As she reached the ground, she looked around.

For a tiny town such as Dayton Falls, it had a rather large train station. She stared at the group of people waiting about on the platform. She had no idea if they were waiting for passengers to arrive or to alight the train themselves.

No one presented themselves to her as Ethan Harper, so she assumed he wasn't here. The best thing to do was find the bakery, and she set off toward the station's exit.

Noticing a wooden bench, Abigail sat herself down and tried to make herself more presentable. Baker or not, this man would be her salvation, and she needed to look at least a little appealing to him.

She pulled off her bonnet and was about to reluctantly fix her hair with her fingers, when she spotted a sign to the privy. She sighed with relief.

Snatching up her carpetbag, she headed in that direction. She hoped there would be a mirror to see what sort of state she was in.

She might be unhappy about marrying a baker, but she still needed to draw his attention. Otherwise he might send her back.

Abigail stared into the tarnished mirror. Her face was covered with black blotches from the soot. That would never do!

She poured some water into the bowl provided and slapped it on her face. It was icy cold, but she had no other option.

Satisfied she'd done all she could with her face, she began to work on her hair. She pulled out the clips that had once held her hair perfectly in place, and rummaged through the carpetbag for her brush.

This was far better than fixing her hair with her fingers.

After a good brushing, she pulled her hair up into a chiffon, then replaced her bonnet on her head.

She already felt much better.

Once she had relieved herself, Abigail was ready to face her groom. But first she had to find the bakery.

She'd been told Dayton Falls was rather small, so it couldn't be that difficult a task, surely?

Giving her gown a last brushing down, she headed back to the platform.

She watched mesmerized as sack after sack of flour was loaded onto a trolley. It was stacked high, and it reminded her of the deliveries they took at her father's bakery.

The young man who was doing most of the hard work looked to be a little under six feet tall. He had chestnut hair, and was very handsome.

She watched as the muscles rippled on his back as he carried each sack over to the trolley. Surely this was not her betrothed? He looked far too young. She guessed around twenty-six.

She gingerly stepped closer. "Mr Harper?" His head swung toward her. "Mr Ethan Harper?" She held her breath waiting for his response.

He turned to stare at her. "No, Miss. I'm his younger brother, Patrick. That's Ethan over there." He pointed toward a small office. Ethan had his back to her, and she couldn't see his face.

If he was anywhere near as handsome as his brother, she'd be more than happy.

"Thank you, Mr Harper," she said, and began to walk away.

He called after her. "You're welcome, Miss."

Her heart thundering in her chest, Abigail braced herself for the meeting. What would he be like, this Ethan Harper? Would he be as handsome as his brother? The most important thing, in Abigail's mind, was that he was a good person.

He turned as she approached and they collided. She squealed.

As she fell backwards from the impact, Abigail closed her eyes, waiting to hit the hard ground. Instead, two strong hands held her by the arms, and pulled her back up.

Her eyes fluttered open and she found herself looking into his flour-covered face.

"I apologize, Miss," he said firmly. "It was totally my fault."

"Yes, it was," she said equally as firmly. "But since you are to be my husband, I shall forgive you."

His eyes opened wide in shock. Was he not aware of her arrival? Or their promise of marriage?

She stepped back, clutching her carpetbag tightly. "You…you are Ethan Harper?" she asked quietly, a quiver in her voice.

He straightened his stance and crossed his arms across his chest. "I am, but I did not promise to marry any woman."

Close to tears, she still had the thought to pull the letter out of her pocket. She handed him the crumpled envelope.

He reached for it with shaking hands, then opened it. His eyes scanned it for only moments. "Ah," he said. "Why didn't you say Miss Bethany had sent you?"

She breathed a huge sigh of relief. Thank goodness she'd been given that letter to bring with her. "You didn't know I was coming? I've spent days on that horrible contraption, and Miss Bethany said..."

He interrupted before she could continue. "I've been at the station most of the day. If she telegraphed, I wasn't around to get it."

Brushing his flour-covered hands against his breeches, he reached out and shook her hand. "You look rather refreshed after such a long trip."

"I managed to clean up when I arrived."

He nodded but didn't answer and Abigail wondered if she lived up to his expectations of his ideal wife.

"Let me take your bag." He reached out and took it without waiting for a response. He frowned and she knew what he was thinking – it was too light to have much in it. She didn't need much. Her father had told her that repeatedly.

"I'm afraid I need to finish up here before I can leave. Why don't you rest on that bench over there?"

The last thing she wanted to do was sit down after enduring it for days on end, but she agreed anyway.

What she really wanted was to get to wherever she was going and have a long hot bath. She felt like a chimney sweep must feel after a day's work.

He escorted her over to the wooden bench. "Have you eaten, Miss…? Forgive me, I don't even know your name." He grinned, as though it was hilarious they were to marry but he didn't know what to call her.

"Abigail Martin," she said quietly, and sat down at his indication. "No, I have not, Mr Harper. The last time I ate was yesterday breakfast when I had a few crackers."

"No wonder you look so pale."

Did she? Abigail hadn't noticed when she looked in the mirror, but she was more concerned with being presentable.

"Patrick!" He called to his brother and waved him over. "Are we done," he asked Patrick. "We need to get back to the store. Miss Martin, er, Abigail hasn't eaten since breakfast yesterday."

She felt herself heat at the embarrassment, and turned her head.

Patrick's smile turned grim. "That's not good," he said. "I'm done here." He began to pull the trolley laden with all the flour and other items they'd received.

Ethan helped Abigail to her feet, not that she needed his help, but it was nice to know she was marrying a gentleman.

Not that he looked much like one right now. His sleeves were rolled up, and not a tie or a jacket was in sight!

His face was covered with splatters of both flour and dirt, but she forgave him being out in public like that. But only because Ethan and Patrick had been loading their baking requirements.

One hand held a bundle of papers, and the other slid up her back and guided Abigail out of the railway station.

She looked back over her shoulder. It seemed larger than the station back home, and it was big. She shook her head – that couldn't be right. They were out in the middle of nowhere in Dayton Falls.

"How long has your bakery been operating?" Abigail asked, not daring to tell him her father's business. The last thing she needed was to be caught up in his business, and being leaned on for constant help in the store.

"We opened last week." He turned to her and smiled. "Business is already very good."

Great. She could see the writing on the wall. When it got too much for him to handle, he'd find a way to get her involved in the business.

Not that she reviled helping out. That wasn't it at all. She just didn't want to be taken advantage of like her father had.

As they made their way along the main street of Dayton Falls, Abigail looked about. It really wasn't very big, but people milled about, going about their business.

Ethan stopped in front of a large store with floor to ceiling windows that showed the café part of the store. He pulled out a bundle of keys and unlocked it.

Her hands reached out to touch the painted sign on the large window. *Dayton Falls Bakery.*

Not very inventive, but it didn't need to be. It said exactly what was needed, and there could be no confusion about the nature of the business.

Her father had chosen Martin's Eatery for his signage and had almost instantly regretted it. Abigail was certain the wording had lost them many a customer. No doubt Peter Jones would eventually change it to something more suitable.

Had he even come through with the payment to buy the bakery? She highly doubted it. He would play her father for a fool given half a chance.

She shook her head trying to shake the thoughts away. The last thing she wanted was to fill her head with memories of Peter Jones and his dishonorable intentions.

Ethan held the door wide for her. "Are you okay? You seem to have paled even more, if that's possible."

He led her across to one of the café tables and sat her down.

Patrick pulled the trolley though the door and out the back to the storeroom, while Ethan headed to the large kitchen and proceeded to make tea for her.

He returned a few minutes later with tea and a buttered scroll. "It's not much, but I'll get you something further shortly. I don't want you passing out on me." He stared at her, waiting for a response.

She took a bite. "Mmmm, this is good," she said, almost adding *even better than my father's*. Luckily she caught her words in time.

"My food is good," he said, pretending to be wounded. "Nothing but the best."

She nodded and took another bite. It really was good, and she could sit here all day, but surely the store would be opening soon? "What time do you open? It must be getting late."

"We open at noon."

Abigail almost choked on her tea. Her father's bakery opened at eight precisely, every day of the week. No wonder he looked tired.

"My father almost killed himself with his bakery," Ethan explained. He began to prepare the food a little after midnight, and worked himself to the ground. The store closed at six, which left little time for rest."

It echoed almost exactly what her father had done for as long as she could remember.

"This way, I get to have a good night's sleep, and have some down time. I want to spend time with my wife, and family if we are blessed to have one."

He grinned at her, and Abigail felt the heat creep up her neck to her cheeks. "Speaking of which, when you are finished eating, you can freshen up, then we'll make our way to the church."

She began to stand, but he waved her down again. "Do finish eating," he said. "I'd never forgive myself if you became ill through lack of nourishment."

He reached into the glass cabinet and retrieved an apple slice. After placing it on a sparkling white plate, he placed it on the table before her, with a similarly shining fork.

She stared at the plate.

"If you don't like it, I can get you something else," he said, a worried look on his face. He totally misunderstood her actions.

The plates in her father's store were old and cracked. These were the most beautiful plates she'd ever seen.

She shook her head and smiled at him. "No, it isn't that. It sounds silly I suppose, but I was admiring your crockery. They're the most beautiful plates I've seen."

He chuckled. "Then you haven't seen many."

She supposed he was right. Her father was too much of a miser to replace the plates, and she doubted Peter Jones would be any better.

"It is easy to see your bakery is new," she said, gazing around and taking in the shiny floor and the cleanliness of the entire store. "Your customers must be enjoying it."

"They're certainly enjoying coming here for coffee and cake. The ladies are making it a regular occurrence, which is good for business."

She nodded. It was exactly what her father needed. Stubborn old mule he was. She'd tried to tell him but he wouldn't listen. The entire situation was becoming quite tiresome.

She swallowed down the last of the apple slice, then gulped the last of the tea. Abigail looked up at him expectantly, and she noticed him staring.

"Is something wrong," she asked, watching him continue to stare at her.

He shook his head as though chasing bad thoughts away. "Nothing is wrong. Nothing at all. I was admiring your beauty," he said genuinely. No one had ever complimented her before, and it felt good.

It also made her blush.

He chuckled. "You are even more beautiful when you blush like that." He had a huge grin on his face, which made her even more embarrassed.

She pushed back her chair and stood, reaching for her soiled dishes out of habit.

"Oh no, don't do that. Allow me," he said, snatching up the few dishes on the table. He carried them to the sink, then returned for Abigail.

He locked the front door to stop early customers, then took her through to the house that was attached to the bakery.

"This is home," he said proudly. "Patrick and I have spent weeks renovating both the bakery and the house."

She glanced around, taking in the features of the house. "You both did a wonderful job," she said, more than a little impressed at their handiwork.

"To be honest, Patrick is a carpenter – it was a huge help." He grinned like a little boy caught with his fingers in the honey jar.

She laughed. It was the first time she'd laughed for a long time, and it felt good.

"Patrick is living with me, er us, at the moment. I hope you don't mind?" He glanced at her waiting for her reaction.

"It's your house, and your decision," she said. Her father had always made the decisions, and Abigail had no choice in anything.

"Once we're married, all that changes," he said. "Here's the bathroom. Freshen up, and we'll go and visit the preacher." He looked down at himself. "I need to clean up too."

He grinned and for the first time she noticed the dimples at either side of his face. Perhaps because he'd made her feel more comfortable and more relaxed, she was noticing more.

He handed Abigail the almost empty carpetbag and left her alone. She closed the bathroom door behind her and pulled off her bonnet. Despite having washed her face at the station, she could still feel the grit on her skin.

It felt horrible.

There was clean water in the beautifully decorated jug, and she poured some into the matching bowl.

Ethan had left a clean towel and face cloth for her, which was very thoughtful.

She soaked the face cloth and held it against her face. It felt so good, so refreshing. She sprinkled her neck with the rosewater she had brought with her. At least she would smell nice.

Her hair wasn't bad, but she brushed it out and redid her chiffon.

The one thing she really wanted to fix was the now dirty gown she wore. She only had two other gowns with her, and they weren't in the best condition, but they were the best she'd had.

She quickly undressed and pulled on a fresh gown. Abigail had no intentions of visiting the house of the Lord in a dirty gown. That would be incredibly disrespectful.

She snatched up her soiled gown and shoved it into the bag. Tomorrow she would wash it.

Try as she might, she couldn't reach the last few buttons to secure them. She would have to ask Ethan to assist her.

She opened the door, to find him loitering in the hallway. "Would you mind," she asked, indicating the buttons. "I can't quite reach."

She turned around and he lifted his hands, but they lingered. He leaned forward and breathed in her fragrance. "You smell nice," he said, approval clearly in his voice.

"It was a last minute addition," she said. "I almost didn't bring it with me."

She felt his fingers fiddling with the buttons. "I'm glad you did," he told her, finally securing the buttons.

When she turned back around she finally noticed he'd put on a vest, tie and a jacket. He cleaned up quite well.

"You have a little…" She reached out and touched his cheek, brushing the flour away. Her fingers tingled where she touched him.

He jolted backwards at the connection. "I'll fix it. Thanks," he said, then disappeared into the bathroom.

He wasn't in there long, when he reappeared. He put out his arm for Abigail to hook her hand through, and they walked toward the kitchen.

"We're off to get married, Patrick. Are you coming?"

There was some rattling, and banging and then he appeared. "I wouldn't miss it for the world," he said, grinning. The two brothers were very much alike, but Abigail knew she'd nabbed the most handsome of the two.

As they strolled toward the church, Abigail noticed the chill in the air. Christmas wasn't far away, and soon it would be cold. Eventually it would snow. The cold would really set in then.

"Here were are." Ethan's distinctive voice rang out in the stillness of the day. "Nervous?"

She nodded. "A little. It's not every day a girl gets to marry a complete stranger."

His smile disappeared. "You don't have to do this," he said quietly. "I won't force you."

She stared into his eyes. "I know," she said equally as soft. "It's just...I hadn't really thought much about it before. Desperation does that to you."

He contemplated her for a few moments. "If you're certain."

She heard Patrick clear his voice behind them. She'd forgotten he was there. As it turned out, their private conversation wasn't so private.

Abigail's heart rate quickened. She wasn't certain she was ready for this.

Chapter Three

Ethan held open the heavy church door for Abigail.

His eyes landed on her beautiful face, then he glanced across at her hair. She'd removed her bonnet when they arrived, and for the first time, he'd had a good look at it.

It was blonde with reddish streaks – it was all he could do not to reach out and touch it.

He was petrified of marrying a stranger, and even before he'd posted the letter to the mail order bride agency, was having second thoughts.

Right up until Abigail arrived this morning, he wondered if he'd done the wrong thing. Chatting to her in the bakery while she ate, his fears had been allayed.

She seemed like a nice person, and it had made him feel more comfortable about the whole *getting married to a stranger* situation.

She looked up at him. He had lingered too long and she was beginning to wonder why. At least he assumed that was how she was thinking.

As he continued to stare, he noticed the fine lines around her eyes. She was tired. Perhaps exhausted. She'd come a long way to marry him.

It made him wonder what she was fleeing from. Inevitably mail order brides were running away from something.

"Is everything alright?"

Her quiet voice brought him out of his wayward thoughts. As a small child his father was forever reprimanding him for daydreaming. He hadn't done it for such a long time.

"Everything is perfectly fine. Are you ready?"

She nodded and proceeded him into the sacred building.

He glanced up and saw the preacher heading toward them. "Good morning, Folks," he said warmly. He stared at them. "You're new in town. I haven't seen you before."

Ethan reached out his hand and introduced himself to the preacher. "Ethan Harper," he said. "I own the new bakery."

Enlightenment filled the preacher's face.

"I've been to your services a few times since I arrived, but sat up the back and snuck out before you had a chance to see me."

The preacher stared him down. "Why on earth would you do that? We're a friendly bunch here in Dayton Falls."

Ethan shrugged his shoulders. He wasn't the most social person. "This is Miss Abigail Martin," he said, changing the subject as quickly as he could. "We would like to be married today. If you have the time, that is."

What he would do if the preacher didn't have time, Ethan wasn't sure. Abigail couldn't stay with him unless they married, and the hotel was far too rowdy to put her up there.

The preacher looked them both up and down.

"Of course," the preacher said, leading them to the front of the church. Patrick trailed behind them.

"Oh, this is my brother, Patrick," he said. "He can be one of the witnesses."

"Let me get my wife as the other witness." He disappeared, but came back shortly. "Hold hands," he instructed the couple. "And move closer together. Do you have a wedding ring?"

Abigail stared at him. "I totally forgot. Should I run out and get one?"

The preacher chuckled. "You'll likely need to order one in. We can proceed without it."

Before he knew it, the ceremony was over. The witnesses signed the paperwork, along with the newly married couple, and they soon left the church.

Once they were outside, Ethan pulled his pocket-watch out of his vest and checked the time. It wouldn't be long and he'd need to open the bakery.

Abigail pulled her bonnet back on her head and they headed off. As they strolled along Main Street, he pointed out the various businesses along the way.

"Can you cook?" He hadn't meant to blurt the question out, but it was too late now. It would be really nice to have a wife who could cook his meals. He was usually too exhausted to do it himself at the end of a busy day.

She grinned. "I can cook," she said, and for some strange reason, he felt there was more to the answer than she was letting on. "Do you have plenty of supplies at home?" She blushed as soon as she asked the question. "I mean, in the house, not the bakery. I know you have plenty there."

"Hmm, not a lot. Perhaps you could check it out when we get back. Anything you need, put on my account at the Mercantile."

She looked down at her empty hand. "I'll come in with you tomorrow, and we'll order a wedding ring."

Her head shot up. "I don't need a wedding ring," she protested. "It's a waste of good money."

"And have people think we're not married? That's not going to happen." She scowled. Was this their first argument? "Let's not argue. These small town people can be vicious, and I don't want you on the receiving end." He reached for her hand, and pulled it to his lips. A tingle ran down his spine.

He heard Patrick clearing his throat behind them. When he looked back over his shoulder, his brother was grinning broadly. "Oh for goodness sakes, Patrick. Act your age." The grin quickly changed to a scowl. "Keep it up and you'll stay at the hotel from now on."

He wasn't sure how long his brother intended to stay, but it wouldn't be too much longer. Patrick had ambitions of his own. Besides, he'd almost finished the work at the bakery.

They stood opposite the bakery, and saw there was already a line of customers waiting. "The bakery seems to be very popular," Abigail said, and it warmed his heart.

"It is. I only hope it continues."

She licked at her lips. "The closer it gets to Christmas, perhaps you can introduce some Christmas fare – Christmas cakes and puddings for instance. I have an old family recipe if you need one."

She suddenly chewed at her bottom lip. *What was she hiding?*

"That sounds like a great idea. We could discuss it later. Right now I have to open the bakery. We'll go in the back way to avoid the crowd."

He led her through the entrance of the house, and left her in the sitting room. He snatched up his apron, and unlocked the front door. More than a dozen people, mostly women, flooded into the store. He stepped back to let them pass, then looked out over the sea of faces. This was exactly what he dreamed about, but there were so many people. How would he cope with them all?

His father had warned him, but he hadn't listened. He mentally slapped himself – this was what he'd wanted, but now he wondered if opening a bakery was the right thing to do.

* * *

Abigail stood in the doorway that adjoined the house and watched as Ethan fumbled with the crowd of customers. At first it was amusing, but it quickly became evident he was overwhelmed.

She felt so bad standing there watching him when she could be helping. She stepped into the store and approached Patrick. "Where can I find a clean apron?"

He stared at her and pointed to a deep drawer. "In there."

"Pen and paper?" He pointed again and she snatched them up. As she tied her apron, she headed out into the store. Ethan did his best to take the orders, but it seemed to be beyond him. How did he think he would manage?

She stood beside him. "I'll take it from here," she said, and he stared at her. "I'll take the orders, and you fulfill them. Understand?"

The customers sitting at the table grinned as he walked away in confusion. "Hello, I'm Abigail," she said, introducing herself. "What would you ladies like today?"

As she wrote their orders down, one woman questioned her. "You're new in town. I'm Mavis Jensen." She reached out her hand.

The other women introduced themselves as Mrs Green, Mrs Jackson, and Mrs Grogan, the doctor's wife.

Abigail knew she'd never remember all their names. Not yet anyway.

"Pleased to meet you all," she said. "I'm Abigail M... er, Harper. Ethan and I married this morning."

The squeals of delight that followed surprised her. He hadn't been in town all that long.

"I told that young man he needed to marry," Mrs Jensen said. "You'll soon settle in. Dayton Falls is a lovely little town."

The other women nodded in agreement.

"Thank you all," she said. "Now let me go back over your orders." She had to get back to business, or she'd never be finished here.

It wasn't long before she delivered the first order to her new husband. She scurried off to take the next table's order before she had to collect and deliver the first.

It was going to be a busy afternoon, but at least she wouldn't be bored. And she'd already made some new friends.

* * *

Ethan stood behind the counter and watched his new bride in amazement.

She looked totally at home, and was far better at taking orders than he was. It was almost as though she'd done it before.

He stared as she strolled toward him, another order torn from the pad, ready to hand over. "They're nice people," she told him quietly. "And they seem pleased you've married. Especially that Mrs Jensen." She grinned.

He chuckled. "She suggested it weeks ago, and hasn't let me forget."

"Is she the reason you sent away…"

He shuffled his feet like a naughty child. "Yes, I guess she is."

She grinned. "Then I should thank her."

Abigail handed over the new order, and snatched up the tray that awaited her. He watched her walk away. She was easy on the eyes, no matter which angle you looked at her.

He heard Patrick move behind him. "You'd better get started on that order, or your missus might ball you out." He laughed and moved out of reach.

He ignored his brother and stared at the order. *Two pots of tea with biscuits, jam, and clotted cream.* The footnote made him smile. *You're doing brilliantly.*

And so was she. Abigail had slotted in as though working in a bakery was second nature.

He glanced up and she was staring at him from across the room. He smiled, acknowledging her footnote.

She smiled back and it warmed his heart.

Was this what being married was like? Stealing glances from across the room?

He suddenly remembered the order and rushed to prepare it before she returned. It wouldn't do to have his new bride chastise him. Especially on their first day of marriage.

Abigail returned with a tray of soiled dishes, and placed it on the sink. He turned to face her, pushing another tray toward her. "This one is ready." He reached out for the order she held in her hand.

Their hands brushed and he shivered. He didn't expect her touch to affect him so much, especially after they'd only met this morning. "Thanks for the vote of confidence," he said, then turned to prepare the next order.

Once the bakery had cleared out to just a few tables in use, Abigail removed her apron. "I'll leave you to it, shall I? I need to organize supper."

He'd already become accustomed to seeing her in the bakery, and didn't want her to leave, but he knew she must. With little in the house pantry, she needed to take stock and go to the Mercantile.

"I'll check back later and see if you need my help."

He reached out and grabbed her hand. "Thank you," he said, bringing her hand to his lips. "Your help made a huge difference."

Heat crept its way up her neck and face. He liked it – it made her look even more beautiful than she already was.

She slowly pulled her hand out of his grip. "You are welcome," she said, then flashed him a smile. Before he could stop her, Abigail was gone. His heart felt hollow as he watched her disappear down the hallway of the attached house.

The bell over the door jingled, and he reluctantly moved to welcome his customers and guide them to a table.

Chapter Four

It had been second nature to waitress on the tables, but too late Abigail realized she may be giving a part of herself away.

The last thing she wanted was to reveal her father's business. She didn't want to be a slave to her husband's bakery like she had been to her father's.

As she made her way down the hallway toward the kitchen, she could feel eyes on her back. She'd felt there was a connection between them when he'd kissed her hand and now she was convinced of it.

Ethan seemed like a gentle man, and had a calming effect on her. It's a pity it didn't help him when his bakery filled with customers. Abigail was very pleased she was able to help him out when it was necessary.

But now she needed to assess the pantry and decide what she would make for supper, and what was needed from the Mercantile, if anything.

If she was lucky, she would manage today, and could put off her visit until tomorrow.

The pantry was quite large. Not that she was surprised. Ethan and Patrick had built the house from scratch, and being a baker, would be generous with the pantry size.

She grabbed a notepad and began to write down the supplies she had, so she could work out what she needed.

There wasn't much. About a cup of flour, some potatoes and onions. In the cooler she found butter and milk. She sniffed the milk – thankfully it was still fine.

Tonight they would have pancakes with fried potatoes and onions, but she would need to get more flour from the bakery. She was certain her husband wouldn't mind.

She searched the kitchen for bowls then headed to the bakery for some additional flour.

The bakery was near-empty when she returned. "Did you scare the customers away?" she asked in jest.

He grinned at her. "I'm thankful for the reprieve. It got mighty busy for a while there." He glanced at the bowl in her hand. "Can I help you with something?"

"I need flour, if I could? There's not much in the house. It seemed silly to go and buy some." She grinned at him and he laughed.

"That would be rather silly," he said, filling the bowl.

She glanced past him. "Ooooh, could I have some of those apples, please?"

He looked over his shoulder. "What are you up to?"

"Apple pie for dessert perhaps? Do you have any clotted cream to spare?"

His eyes lit up. "I'm already enjoying having a wife. I hate to admit it, but we've just been eating the leftovers from the bakery."

"Oh, you haven't!" At first she was shocked, then realized after a long day in the bakery, he'd likely had enough of slaving over a hot stove. That was about to change.

He filled the bowl with flour, and handed over the apples. She placed them in her apron pocket. As she moved to leave, he held her by the shoulders and moved closer.

Her heart thudded in her chest.

Ethan leaned in and gave her a quick kiss on the cheek. "Thank you," he said gently, then let his hands drop to his sides.

It was strange, but she felt disappointed he'd only kissed her on the cheek. But she simply nodded then made her way back to the kitchen.

Abigail glanced around the room. This was a far bigger kitchen than she'd had at her father's home. His was not purpose built. It was a cottage her parents had acquired before she was born. It had been their first home as a married couple, and had become their permanent home.

He had long spoken of finding something larger, but never did. When her mother died, he'd never mentioned it again. Abigail hadn't dared bring it up.

The kitchen she was forced to cook in was tiny. Their cottage was tiny. Truth be told, it was fine for a married couple with no children, but not for a family.

This house of Ethan's was wonderful. It was definitely built with a family in mind.

Abigail felt her face heat at the thought of having a family with Ethan.

As she peeled the potatoes she wondered what it would be like having children of her own. It was something that had never entered her mind before. She'd been far too busy to even think about it, but there was no one she'd ever wanted to have a family with before.

Ethan Harper was a fine specimen of a man. She would be very happy to have a child with him. Her face heated again and felt as though it was burning.

She heard sounds behind her and spun around.

Ethan stood there grinning at her. "What have you been thinking about," he asked. "Your cheeks are red."

It only served to make her even more embarrassed. Her hands flew to her cheeks. She turned back to the counter and continued peeling potatoes. "Nothing," she said quietly, and Ethan laughed again.

"If you say so. I only came in to make sure you found everything you needed."

She nodded. "I have, thank you."

He left the room and she felt two feet tall. He came in at the worst possible time. Abigail groaned. Once she'd finished with the potatoes, she diced them ready to fry. She then peeled the onions, and lastly made the pancake batter and sat it aside.

This was her mother's favorite recipe. She'd taught Abigail how to make it when she was very young.

She blinked back the tears that threatened to flood her face. She missed her mother so much. But now was not the time to dwell on the past. She had two hungry men to feed.

She'd made the pastry earlier, and only needed to peel and slice the apples for the pie. Feeling quite proud of herself, she set out the plates ready for serving once supper was ready.

Checking the kitchen drawers, she found a checkered table cloth, and placed it on the table, then set it for three. She placed the potatoes and onions in the heavy frying pan, and stood over them, stirring often.

The last thing she needed was her first meal to be burned.

Mother would be proud of her, she was certain. If only she had lived long enough to see Abigail married and happy.

Well, she was married, but whether she would be happy was yet to be seen.

Chapter Five

Abigail placed the food in front of them, then sat down. Ethan reached for her hand at the same time Patrick did. He noted her surprise.

They bowed their heads and said Grace. As she looked up, Abigail seemed happy, relaxed even. "It's a long time since I've said thanks for food," she said softly. "Father is not a believer. When my mother died, all sensibility seemed to leave him."

"I'm sorry for your loss," Ethan said, not sure what else he should say.

She brushed her hand across in front of her. "It was a long time ago. Please, eat before it goes cold."

The two men tucked in. "This is good," Patrick said, his mouth full of food.

"You're a lout, Patrick. But he's right, the food is delicious." He reached for her hand and squeezed it. "Thank you."

No matter how much he resisted, every time he touched his wife, a shiver ran down his spine.

Surely it was purely from having a woman in the house?

She suddenly jumped up from the table, and he frowned. "Dessert," she said, and he understood. She didn't want it to burn.

He didn't want it to burn either. If the main course was anything to go by, dessert would be delicious.

Ethan craned his neck to see. It looked perfect from where he sat. In the short time he'd known her, Abigail had strived for perfection, so the pie would be no different.

He breathed in the enticing aroma. "It looks and smells amazing."

Patrick continued to feed his face, so Ethan kicked him under the table. Patrick scowled at him, then finally understood. "Oh. Yes. Yes, it does. It smells amazing."

It was Ethan's turn to scowl. His brother was nothing but an insensitive oaf at times. He sighed.

"Finish your food before it goes cold," he told his wife, patting her chair. She smiled at him, and his heart fluttered.

He was acting like an adolescent schoolboy the first time he kissed a girl. He needed to get over himself.

Ethan so badly wanted to ask why Abigail had fled her home to marry a complete stranger, but now was not the time. She needed time to settle in, and if she deemed him worthy, perhaps one day she would tell him.

He marveled at her beauty, at her beautiful hair – it wasn't the first time he'd caught himself staring at it. It seemed to mesmerize him, and usually at the worse possible times.

Right now was no different. "Is everything alright?"

He straightened his shoulders and glanced at her. "Perfectly. Why would you think otherwise?"

She frowned and turned her head away. "No reason." She shook her head as she spoke the words. There was so much he wanted to say to her, but not with his brother sitting beside him.

He had never wished for privacy so much as he did at this moment. The beautiful creature sitting next to him was his wife and he wanted to learn more about her.

His wife!

The realization seemed to finally come to him, and he wasn't unhappy about it either. "I'll serve up dessert," she said, reaching for his empty plate.

His hand snaked around her wrist. "Thank you," he said quietly, wanting to say more, but biding his time.

"You don't have to keep thanking me," she said gently. "It's my job."

He gasped. Was that what she thought? That he'd written for a mail-order bride because he needed what amounted to a slave?

Disappointment filled him. He had never thought of a wife that way, but if he was truthful with himself, he did want to a wife to help him in the bakery when needed. A hot supper every night was an added bonus.

His thoughts made him pause. Abigail would not become his slave. She was his wife, not someone to order around and fulfill his every wish.

He watched her as she served up the food. She'd done this before – and not just in a home kitchen. When she placed the pie in front of him, his suspicions were confirmed.

Each slice was cut to perfection, the portions even, and the amount of clotted cream on each slice perfectly aligned with the others.

He stared at her. *What secret was she hiding?*

For now he would enjoy the moment, but he vowed to find out the truth.

* * *

Patrick and Ethan were relaxing in the sitting room, while Abigail finished up the dishes.

Ethan had offered to help, but she'd denied his offer – she'd been doing this very thing for years without assistance. She didn't need help now she'd told him.

After packing everything away where it belonged, she pulled her apron over her head. Next on her list was to clean the tables and chairs in the bakery. Normally she would have already cleaned in there, but today was all out of sorts.

She was certain Ethan would understand.

She could hear the men talking and laughing in the sitting room. No doubt the fire was burning, since it was quite chilly. Not to worry, she would warm up during the cleaning. At least that's what her father always said.

Not that he'd been proven to be right. Not always anyway.

Heading toward the adjoining door, bucket of soapy water in her hands, she was as quiet as she could be, not wanting to disturb the men with their conversation.

When she arrived there, however, the door was stuck. Abigail turned the doorknob several times, and even rattled the door, but it wouldn't budge.

"What are you doing?" Her husband stood behind her, a scowl on his face. She cowered down from him. He took a step back, now frowning.

"I, I'm trying to open the door. I need to scrub the tables and chairs."

He reached out and took the bucket from her hands, handing it over to Patrick who had now joined them. His hands sat gently on her arms. "What you need to do is join us in the sitting room."

He studied her face, and she wondered what he was trying to determine. "The tables need to be scrubbed. And the chairs," she said, almost desperately. "Everything must be clean for tomorrow's customers."

He shook his head and tears filled her eyes. She blinked them back – her new husband was not going to see her distress. "I, I should have done it before supper, but I ran out of time."

His arms snaked around her back and he pulled her closer. "Dear Abigail," he whispered. "What have they done to you?"

The movement of his hands circling over her back was soothing, and she sank into him. Her arms slowly went around his waist.

Tears slid down her face. She was beginning to wonder the same thing herself. Over time she'd changed from being a treasured daughter to being a slave to her father's business.

She lifted her hand to wipe the tears before they were seen, but it was too late. Ethan's arms slid underneath her and he carried her to the bedroom, where he laid her gently on the bed.

Patrick followed, a bemused look on his face, but Ethan slammed the bedroom door in his face. "That boy needs to grow up," he said under his breath, then looked down at her with sadness.

His fingers gently caressed her face, and she immediately felt relaxed. Abigail looked up at him, her eyes beginning to close. He pulled off her shoes, then undid the fastenings at the back of her gown. He helped her slide in under the covers.

It had been such a long day, and she could barely keep her eyes open. Ethan leaned in and brushed his lips across hers. "I'll leave the room so you can change into your nightgown."

She appreciated the thought, but she had no nightgown.

Abigail slipped out of her gown, leaving on only her chemise and drawers. She hung her gown up in the wardrobe and slipped in under the covers once more.

Her eyes fluttered closed the moment her head hit the pillow.

* * *

"I don't know what she'd been through, but she's traumatized," Ethan said to his brother as his finger pounded Patrick's chest. "You need to be more sensitive to other people's feelings."

Patrick stared at him momentarily, then chuckle. Ethan scowled. "It's not a joke. Change your attitude or you can get accommodation at the hotel."

That wiped the smile off his face. "You don't mean that, surely?" He plonked down into a chair in the sitting room. "I mean, I'm blood. I helped you build this house, the bakery…you, you don't even know Abigail." He looked more wounded by the minute.

"You are blood, there's no doubting it, but Abigail is my wife. And she clearly needs looking after." He sat opposite his brother, but wasn't feeling very accommodating toward him right now. "You've been a tremendous help, Patrick, and I truly appreciate it. But I can't allow you to be anything but respectful toward my wife."

He watched as the tiniest beginning of a smile passed his brother's lips. It was gone as quickly as it appeared.

"You're serious, aren't you?" He frowned.

Ethan straightened in his chair. "I most certainly am. And now there's a woman in the house, there are new rules. Especially no walking around half naked. Or using bad language."

Patrick pouted. "I thought being married was meant to be fun."

"You're not the one married though, are you?" Ethan grinned briefly, then got out of his chair. "I need to check on Abigail. I'll say goodnight now. See you in the morning."

"Sure."

Ethan stood and was about to leave the room when Patrick spoke. "I'm really sorry," he said quietly, and sounded like he meant it.

Patrick was clearly unhappy, but Abigail had to be his priority from now on. His brother was old enough and independent enough to look after himself. He could stay for as long as he abided by the rules. Besides, he'd been paying him wages – as much as a complete stranger would have been paid, so he needn't feel bad about making him leave if it came to that.

Ethan made his way to the bedroom and carefully opened the door. Abigail was asleep under the covers. At least she appeared to be.

He closed the door quietly and gazed down at her.

This morning he was living the life of a bachelor who had recently begun his own business in a new town. Tonight he was a married man trying to work out what had happened to his wife to make her behave in such a strange way.

He stood watching her gentle breathing for some time, was mesmerized by it. By her. Abigail was strong and helpful one minute, and weak and broken the next.

Her actions were confusing, but he vowed to get to the bottom of it.

She gently groaned in her sleep and rolled over, her streaked hair spreading out over the pillow. It looked so soft, and it took all his effort not to reach out and touch it. Touch her.

He pulled the covers up over her almost bare shoulders, then made his way to the other side of the bed. He sat on the easy chair, which was in the corner near the window, and began to undress.

Ethan hadn't planned on having a wife tonight, but he wasn't unhappy about it either. Abigail was very likeable, and was obviously used to hard work. It would be nice to have a helping hand, but she needed to slow down.

He pulled his nightgown up over his head, and eased himself into the bed trying not to disturb her. Abigail rolled over again, this time facing away from him. It was strange having another person in the bed with him, but he was sure he'd get used to it.

He closed his eyes and was soon asleep.

When Ethan awoke it was to an empty bed. He reached across where his wife had slept, and the bedding was slightly warm. The indent of the pillow where her head had rested was still there.

He leaned over. Her fragrance still lingered. He liked it. All of it.

Shoving the covers back, he climbed out of bed and was greeting by the chilly morning air. The closer it got to Christmas, the worse it would be. Thank goodness he'd had the forethought to put a fireplace in the main bedroom.

From now on, he'd ensure it was burning when they went to bed. At least they wouldn't have such a rude awakening as today.

He quickly dressed and made his way to the kitchen. The aroma of bacon and eggs assailed his senses before he even reached his destination.

The warmth of the sitting room fire and the wood stove hit him as he walked down the hallway, and he instinctively knew Abigail had been up for quite some time already.

As he entered the kitchen, she was a sight to behold. She looked far less tired this morning than she had yesterday, and the pretty salmon colored gown she wore matched her hair perfectly.

"Good morning," she said sweetly, then stepped forward and gently kissed his cheek.

He pulled her into a hug, and she relaxed into him. "Good morning. I trust you slept well? You look much better today."

"Thank you. I did." She pulled out of his grip and attended to the food sizzling on the stove. "Your coffee is on the table, and your meal is almost ready. Do sit down." She indicated the table, so he did as he was instructed.

Patrick appeared just moments later. "Good morning," he said, then looked to Ethan as if questioning his standing in regard to accommodation.

"Your coffee is on the table," Abigail told him sweetly. "Breakfast will be served in just a moment."

Patrick glanced across at him. Ethan shrugged. He might give off a façade of nonchalance, but deep down he was concerned.

She placed food in front of each of them, then put her own at her setting. Then Abigail sat. She reached out her hands to them, this time prepared to give thanks for their food.

She closed her eyes and bowed her head, and Ethan said a prayer of thanks.

She smiled coyly as they heaped their praises on her cooking, but jumped up to clear the table the moment they were finished.

Ethan stood and came up behind her, ready to help with the dishes. She shook her head. "I don't need help," she said. "You get on with your baking. I'll be out soon."

No matter how much he protested, she insisted. It seem to distress her to be told no, so he let it go.

Glancing in the sitting room on his way through, Ethan discovered the fire was roaring. Unlocking the adjoining door, he grabbed for an apron, ready to begin the day's work.

He checked the temperature of the ovens before anything else, then measured out the flour and other ingredients.

Kneading the bread on the spotless countertop had always been a time of reflection for Ethan, and today was no different.

His new wife had him somewhat bamboozled. One minute she was relieving him of his duties in the bakery and taking orders, and only hours later she was a blubbering mess.

There had to be a reason.

Right at this moment, the best thing he could do was keep an eye on her, and ensure she wasn't overloaded. Even if that was of her own hand.

The adjoining door opened, and Abigail quickly joined him. She reached into the drawer and pulled out a fresh apron. "What can I do to help?"

"I'm nearly done with the first batch of bread, but if you could check the stocks of cakes and slices, it would be really helpful."

She grabbed a notepad and pen, but before she could leave, he grabbed her gently by the wrist and pulled her close. Ethan looked down into her face. "I'm so glad you came," he said softly.

At first she looked up at him, but then she looked down, as though she was ashamed. "I am too," she whispered, then pulled out of his grip and headed to the display counter.

He could have held her like that all morning. And for once, he wished he had no customers, no one to distract him from his wife.

He watched as Abigail noted down what supplies were there, and handed him the list. It was as though their brief encounter had never occurred.

She rounded on the tables, checking their cleanliness. This is what had distressed her so much last night. She glanced up at him. "Not bad," she said. "But I'll give them a quick scrub. Customers can't eat at dirty tables."

She left the room, presumably to retrieve a bucket of soapy water. Ethan put the bread in the ovens then checked the tables for himself. He couldn't see anything, and ran his hands across the tables.

Nothing. Not a thing.

Abigail returned and began scrubbing the tables, drying them with a clean kitchen towel. She moved from table to table, then started over with the chairs.

"When was the floor last washed?" she asked firmly.

He glanced up from kneading his next batch of bread. "I washed it last night before I closed up for the evening."

She nodded, then dropped to her knees. Abigail ran her hands across the clean floor. "It's not perfect, but close." She pulled herself into a standing position again, then washed her hands at the bakery sink.

Ethan removed the first batch of bread from the oven and tipped the loaves out of their tins. No sooner were they in the large sink, than Abigail was scrubbing them.

He came up behind her, brandishing a clean dish towel. "I'll dry," he said, then moved closer while she washed.

Being close to her was his new favorite thing to do. Prior to Abigail arriving, baking and building up his business was where all his energy had been focused.

She glanced at him over her shoulder and smiled. He decided she was as happy about his nearness as he was. She passed over the first clean bread tin and he took it from her hands.

Their hands brushed, and a thrill went up his arm. *Did she feel that too?* He glanced at her and she was staring at him, eyes wide.

"Why don't you get back to your baking, and I'll deal with the tins?" she suggested, and all he could do was nod.

It was a blessed relief to have help in the bakery. Already it was easier for him, and she'd been here such a short time.

With the bakery cleaned and the loaves of bread cooling on the racks, Ethan began making slices and cakes. They'd been extremely popular so far, and had sold out most days.

They were only weeks from Christmas and his mind went back to Abigail's suggestion of producing Christmas fare.

Dare he risk making such expensive items this soon after opening the doors?

"Abigail," he said gently. "We didn't get to discuss your idea."

She turned to face him. Why did she seem so surprised at his comment?

"Idea?" Had she really forgotten?

"You mentioned making Christmas cakes and puddings to sell in the bakery."

She pulled her bottom lip in with her teeth. "Oh. Yes, I did."

He frowned.

"I have an old family recipe," she said. "It would be an expensive item to make, but I'm willing to bet it will be popular with your customers."

He frowned again. "How expensive?"

She grabbed a sheet of paper and wrote down the recipe. Ethan checked it over. "I don't think it would be too bad, but we'd have to get some supplies from the Mercantile in the beginning."

Abigail looked thoughtful. "You could make one and sell slices of it with coffee. That way people would get to try it before they bought a whole one."

It was an excellent idea. He pulled his pocket-watch out and checked the time, then pulled his apron over his head. "Let's go to the Mercantile now. I'll make the first one shortly since it takes so long to cook, and we'll serve it tomorrow."

They would also buy a nightgown for Abigail, and whatever other clothing she needed, he told her.

She pulled off her apron, and they went to the Mercantile together.

Chapter Six

While Ethan prepared his first Christmas cake, Abigail took orders from the customers and also prepared and served them.

She could see it pained Ethan to have her doing everything, but it didn't bother her at all. She was very used to running a bakery practically by herself.

Father did most of the baking in the early morning, then often left her alone for the rest of the day. Theirs was a busy store, and at times she really struggled. But this bakery was quiet in comparison.

The bell over the door jingled and she turned. "Hello Mrs Jensen," she said, priding herself for remembering the older woman's name. She guided the woman and her companions to a seat near the fire. "What would you like today, ladies?"

After taking their orders, Abigail leaned in conspiratorially. "Tomorrow we'll have fresh Christmas cake on offer," she said quietly, putting her fingers across her lips as though it was a huge secret. She knew word would get around far quicker this way than any advertising Ethan might undertake.

Mrs Jensen winked at her. "We'll definitely be back tomorrow then," she said, looking around the table. The other women nodded.

It was all Abigail could do to stop herself from grinning. She understood how to run a business, and she knew how to get people to spread the word. She only hoped Ethan would be pleased.

She made up their orders and delivered them to the table. More customers arrived as she handed them out.

Ethan leaned over the counter. "I am nearly done," he said quietly. "I'll take over after that."

But she wouldn't allow it. She would continue to help him in the bakery as long as she could. Another hour or so and she would need to see to their supper, and would come back after that.

She'd done it for so many years it was second nature. Except of course for the days her father disappeared, which was most days. Then she had to stay all day and improvise supper.

She seated the latest customers then went behind the counter to make up their order. Ethan pulled her aside where the customers couldn't see them.

"Thank you," he said softly. "You've been amazing. I don't know how to thank you."

She frowned. "You don't have to thank me. I'm your wife," she said. "I'll do whatever I can to help make your business successful."

"Abigail," he said gently. "You've already done so much." He pulled her close against him, and his hands went up her back. He rubbed gentle circles across her back and she didn't want to move.

She always felt so loved and wanted when he embraced her like this, felt like they'd been together forever.

The bell over the door jingled again and she reluctantly stepped out of his arms.

"Good afternoon," she said, greeting their latest customers. "Let me guide you to your table."

When she took the orders to Ethan, he pulled her out of sight of the customers and hugged her. Had he sensed she needed it? Or did he need the affection as much as she did?

She honestly didn't care – finally she felt like she was wanted, and not a burden.

She pulled out of his grip and peeked at the Christmas cake cooking in the oven. "Smells good," she said, and Ethan leaned in over her shoulder.

"Mmmm, it does. Let's hope the customers like it." His arm went up around her shoulders. "That was a great suggestion," he told her. "You're a great asset to this business."

Disappointment filled her. Was that all she was to him? An asset?

She wanted to be more than an asset – she wanted to be a special part of his life.

He stepped back from the oven, and turned her in his arms, then leaned down and brushed his lips across hers. Ever so lightly, but it was enough to send a thrill down her spine.

"I, I had better get back to the customers," she said, then scurried away. If she wasn't careful, she might end up liking her husband far more than she'd intended.

Theirs was meant to be a marriage of convenience, and nothing more.

As the thought entered her mind, her heart thudded. Was that really what she wanted? A marriage of convenience?

That was certainly Ethan's wish. His letter stated he wanted a wife to help him in the bakery and produce children for him. He couldn't have been any clearer than that.

So why did he go on with the pretense of wanting to be more than mere friends?

It didn't make any sense whatsoever.

Before Abigail could analyze the situation any further, she had to attend to her customers. Soiled dishes sat on the tables, and that wouldn't do.

* * *

They sat around the table eating.

Ethan's Christmas cake looked to be perfect. They'd find out for sure in the morning when they cut it ready to sell.

Tonight they were both exhausted – they'd been rushed off their feet today. As much as Ethan wanted his business to grow, he didn't want it so busy they couldn't keep up.

He reached across the table and covered Abigail's hand. "Thank you for all your help today," he said gently.

His wife nodded. She'd told him repeatedly there was no need to thank her, but he still wanted to. One thing he'd learned living with his father, and later becoming his apprentice, was voicing your appreciation was important.

Not to the person voicing it, but the person on the receiving end.

It was a thankless job working in a bakery, and when you weren't being paid wages, it was even worse.

"I can't wait to cut the cake in the morning, and see how it came out."

She grinned at him. "Hopefully it's perfect. I've been rounding up customers all day for your Christmas cake special tomorrow."

He suddenly felt alarmed. *What if the cake turned out to be inedible?*

He groaned.

She squeezed his hand. "Don't stress. I'm certain it will be perfect. I have made hundreds of them, and never had a single failure."

Hundreds? Why would she have made hundreds?

He had the beginning of a headache.

Ethan glanced at her. She was chewing on her bottom lip. Again. What secret was Abigail hiding from him?

"Is there something you want to tell me?"

He was answered with a frown. She shook her head and jumped up from the table. He held tight to her hand.

"I need to take the cherry cobbler from the oven."

He reluctantly loosened his grip.

Patrick looked from one to the other of them, but said not a word. Ethan shot him a glance, warning him not to interfere.

Perfectly portioned slices of the pie with their equally perfect clotted cream was placed in front of each of them.

Ethan leaned in. "It smells amazing. Where did you learn to cook like this?" He glanced across to his wife, who was once again chewing on her bottom lip.

He squeezed his eyes tightly, then looked up at her. He couldn't put his finger on it, but she was hiding something.

Perhaps she'd worked in a café or a diner? He shook his head. That didn't sound feasible. Not unless she was the cook there.

He dearly wanted to ask her, but not in front of Patrick. As much as he loved his brother, he really wanted privacy. There was so much he wanted to know, needed to know, but didn't want to confront her or embarrass her in front of his brother.

She sat back down at the table and threw him a quick smile. He lifted his spoon and took a mouthful of the delicious smelling dessert.

He glanced up at her. "You've outdone yourself this time," he said genuinely. "This is the best cherry cobbler I've ever had." He took another mouthful.

Patrick joined in. "It's the best I've eaten too."

"Thank you," she said coyly. "I've been cooking since my mother died some years ago." She nibbled on her bottom lip again.

That might be true, and likely it was, but he was still convinced it was only half the story.

When they'd finished eating, the men moved into the sitting room. He'd again offered to help with the dishes, but Abigail would have none of it.

The moment they were settled, Patrick glanced across at him, a frown on his face. "I've almost finished the fit-out for the bakery," he said. "If it isn't a problem for you, I'll leave once it's done."

He appeared somewhat stressed, why, Ethan had no idea. "That's perfectly fine. It was always temporary. What will you do?"

Patrick perked up a bit. "I've had an offer of work in Great Falls. The town is expanding beyond expectations, and new buildings are needed."

His heart thudded. The brothers had rarely been apart in their entire lives, but it was too good an opportunity to miss out on. "I'll be sorry to see you go, but that's excellent news, a great opportunity for you." It truly was. Patrick had been working toward this for most of his adult life. "When do you have to leave?"

Patrick swallowed. "I start work on Monday. It doesn't give me much time, but I'll finish your job first, then leave Thursday. It will give me time to find somewhere to live before I have to start."

Ethan leapt out of his chair and shook his brother's hand. Patrick stood and the two men hugged. They jumped apart when Abigail stepped into the room.

"Uh, sorry. I can go…" She turned to leave.

"Don't go, this affects you too. Patrick has secured an exciting position in Great Falls. He'll be leaving us in a few days."

Was that relief he saw on her face?

He had to admit it would be better with only the two of them. They were newlyweds after all. Newlyweds with no privacy, and no chance to talk about the things they needed to discuss.

She nodded. "Congratulations. You must be thrilled." She stepped up to him and gave him a quick hug. "I'll be sorry to see you go."

The last thing Ethan had expected was for his wife to be hugging his brother.

Patrick glanced across at him and grinned. Jealousy was not something Ethan had experienced before, but watching his wife hug another man, it quickly moved to the surface. To make it worse, Patrick was enjoying himself.

He reached out and pulled Abigail to him, wrapping his arms around her shoulders. It was an act of possession, there was no doubt about it.

"We're going to miss you," he said, squeezing her shoulders. "But it is important for your future." He turned to Abigail. "I'm going to cut a slice off that cake. I want to ensure it's flawless. If not, I still have time to bake another one."

He watched as she frowned. "I know I can't convince you otherwise, but it will be cooked to perfection. Trust me."

Trust her? Right now he wasn't sure what to think – she was hiding something, and Ethan had convinced himself they weren't insignificant in the scheme of things. No, the secrets Abigail was hiding were big ones. Perhaps even important to their future.

"Oh, alright then. Cut a small slice off the side. You'll see I'm right." She pulled out of his grip and headed toward the bakery.

He had to unlock the door for her to enter.

The Christmas cake was on the counter cooling, a clean kitchen towel covering it. He lit a lantern and snatched up a large cook's knife, then carefully cut a slice from the end.

He held his breath – was this going to be the disaster he feared?

"Ha! See, I told you it would be fine."

He glanced up at his wife. She was right – it was absolutely perfect, and moist. It was the most moist Christmas cake he'd ever had the good fortune to make.

He pulled her close and kissed her forehead. "You were right. I should have trusted your judgement."

"Yes you should have," she said, not unkindly. "Perhaps next time you will."

Having been admonished in no uncertain terms, he covered the cake again and followed her out of the bakery.

He locked the adjoining door again, and decided it was time for bed.

It would be nice if he could get to hold his wife tonight. So far he'd not had that luxury.

* * *

Abigail snuggled down into the bed in her new nightgown.

Ethan had lit the fire earlier, so the room was warm and toasty by the time she entered.

So far she'd avoided the inevitable by ensuring she was asleep when her new husband came to bed. He was not demanding, but eventually things would change.

She knew they would.

Voices drifted along the hallway, and she assumed the two men were saying goodnight. Patrick would be gone soon – Abigail wasn't sure if that was a good thing or not. At the moment she was able to bide her time. Ethan hadn't asked the questions she knew he was desperate to ask.

Every time she let something slip, she could see it on his face. The unanswered questions. The suspicion. The desperation that his eyes displayed.

She would have to tell him, but if he was unhappy about her deception, she'd rather it happen when Patrick was not around.

The door to their room opened and her husband entered. She stared up at him. For not the first time she noticed what a wonderful specimen he was.

Ethan had muscles where most men didn't. It came from lifting the sacks of flour, and from kneading the bread each day.

As he closed the door he began to unfasten the buttons on his shirt. She blinked at his bare chest, and the hair she could see there.

Abigail closed her eyes, then heard him chuckle. "Have you never seen a bare chest before?" he asked, still chuckling at her actions.

She sat upright in the bed. "Of course not! How dare you suggest otherwise."

Despite her protests, he continued removing his clothing. She gasped at the sight before her, then covered her mouth with her hands. Her eyes followed his every move.

She knew she shouldn't, but she couldn't help but stare. He stood at the end of the bed grinning at her, then sat down beside her.

"In case you've forgotten, we are married," he said gently, lifting her hand to his lips. "It is totally acceptable to see me naked."

He wasn't quite naked, but he certainly wasn't far from it. She felt the heat creep up her neck and face. How red she must be!

He laughed again. "My sweet and innocent wife," he said, laying her back down, and brushing her lips with his own.

Abigail liked it when he kissed her. It felt good, and it sent a shiver down her spine. He was special, this husband of hers, in so many ways.

He went to the other side of the bed and climbed in, shutting down the lantern.

"What about your nightgown," she asked, horrified to think he would be laying next to her in just his drawers.

At least his did wear his drawers.

The thought entered her head before she could push it away. She felt herself blush again.

She rolled over to face the door, her back to her husband. Her eyes began to drift closed. It had been a big day, a busy day, and she was beyond tired. She needed to sleep.

Her eyes shot open when his arm snaked over her hips and cradled her belly. She reached up to push his hand away, but paused when he wriggled across to her side of the bed.

"Do you mind?" he asked gently.

She couldn't say no. He'd been so kind to her, taking her in. Giving her a place to stay, and a reason to get up each day.

"I don't mind," she said in a whisper, and he tightened his grip.

It felt nice lying there with her husband, feeling his muscles against her back. She didn't know it could be like this being married. But she knew there was more to it than only being held. Abigail wasn't sure what she thought about that.

His lips gently kissed her neck, and her hand reached up and touched his cheek. His skin was soft, but the stubbled scratched her fingers.

"I'm not sure..." she began, but soon changed her mind.

Chapter Seven

As the sunlight crept through the curtains in the bedroom, Abigail slid quietly out of bed.

Last night had been an eye opener for her – without a mother to talk to about such things, she had no idea what to expect.

She sat quietly on the edge of the bed and reached for the robe Ethan had purchased for her. She squealed as a hand reached out and pulled her back into bed.

Abigail shook her head. "I have to get up," she said, pushing his hand away. "I have far too much to do to be…"

She didn't finish the sentence as he continued to try and coerce her. "Seriously. I have work to do." She pulled away and headed toward the bathroom.

Today would be busy. She'd seen to that by planting ideas in their customer's heads. Christmas cake with clotted cream on the side. An absolute delicacy, she'd told them. They could have it with tea or coffee for a discounted price.

To top it all off, orders could be placed that day.

These were all tactics her father used in his bakery, and it had been thriving for many years. She was the one who baked the Christmas cakes. Father didn't have time for such frivolity – he'd told her time after time – but put his hand out for the profits. Abigail had never seen even a cent of it.

At least this time she would be helping her husband, and the profits would be put to good use. She had long suspected her father of gambling, but had no proof. She wondered if that's how Peter Jones came to have the promise of marrying her.

Did her father gamble her life away? The thought brought tears to her eyes.

As she headed to the kitchen, she wiped at her eyes and didn't see Ethan step out of the bedroom. They collided and she ended up on the hallway floor.

She squealed.

Patrick ran from his room in only his drawers. Ethan glared at him. "What did I tell you?"

He backed up. "Sorry, I heard Abigail scream, and thought I'd better check on her."

She stared up at him, averting her eyes from his near-nakedness. "Thank you, Patrick. That was very thoughtful of you. Your brother and I collided. I'll be alright."

Without warning, Ethan reached under her and picked her up, carrying Abigail to the bed, which was only a matter of steps away. She was exasperated. "Put me down," she said under her breath. "I am quite capable of walking."

He glanced at her. "You don't know that. Let me check you over."

"Seriously," she said. "I am perfectly fine."

He laid her on the bed and began to feel up and down her legs. The action made her heart thud in her chest.

She glanced up to see Patrick standing in the doorway, a grin on his face.

"Can you close the door," she whispered. Ethan looked back over his shoulder.

He kicked the door then turned back to what he was doing. "I'll be glad when he's gone."

Abigail gasped. "You don't mean that."

He rubbed his hands across his unshaven face. "No, I don't, but he's so…annoying at times. Besides," he said dramatically. "I want you all to myself."

She reached up and ran her fingers along his chin. The action sent shivers down her spine. Ethan leaned in and kissed her – gently at first, but then the kiss became more urgent.

"Ethan," she whispered. "This is not the time."

He lifted his head slightly and glanced at her, shaking his head. "No, you're right," he said, regret clearly evident in his voice. "But I reserve the right to continue tonight."

She said nothing, but inwardly, warmth invaded her whole body.

He grinned then continued to check her over.

"I told you I was fine," she said, sliding off the bed. "Now let me organize breakfast."

Ethan stared at her, but didn't say another word.

"I'm making scrambled eggs and bacon this morning," she said as she opened the bedroom door. When she arrived in the kitchen, Patrick was stoking the fire. The kettle was close to boiling, and she pulled the mugs down out of the cupboard, then reached for the frying pan.

"It's a pity you're taken," he said. "I could do with a wife like you. I can't cook to save myself," he said as he chuckled.

"She *is* taken," Ethan said firmly as he entered the kitchen and overheard the conversation. "This little lady is mine." He wrapped his arms around her, and despite being disturbed in her quest to prepare breakfast, Abigail didn't mind in the slightest.

It felt good to be wanted, to be cared for, and to be needed. Perhaps one day Ethan would even come to love her.

Not in the traditional way, but after some time he might become accustomed to having her there and find himself having a special connection with her. Much like her parents had before her mother had died.

She pulled out of his arms and reached for the eggs. Breaking them into a porcelain bowl, she took a fork from the drawer and pulled the milk from the cooler. Ethan handed her the salt and pepper.

They were a good team. Even in the bakery they worked well together. Perhaps that's where their relationship lay. She didn't care provided they continued to get on together, and he wasn't abusive toward her.

He hadn't been so far, so there was really no reason why Abigail should even think it.

As each piece of bread was toasted, Ethan buttered it and placed it on the plates. Soon the rest of the food was ready, and they bowed their heads and said a prayer of thanks.

"I'm going to miss this," Patrick said. "Your cooking, I mean."

"Perhaps you can find somewhere that provides meals with the lodgings," Ethan declared. It made perfect sense.

"That's a great idea, but nothing will compare to the amazing food Abigail has been making."

Ethan glanced at her. "He's right, you're an amazing cook." He shoved a forkful of food into his mouth. "This is delicious."

Abigail was grinning, she knew she was. But how did you not when two grown men sang your praises for cooking something so basic as scrambled eggs?

"You're both wonderful," she said quietly. "The truth is, anyone can make this – even a child."

Ethan's head spun around and he frowned. "That is so far from the truth it's not funny," he said firmly. "We've both tried making it and burned it to a crisp."

"Another time it was full of egg shells," Patrick offered. "Plus we burned the toast."

Ethan pulled a face. "What about the time it was cooked on the outside, and raw on the inside?"

She put her hands up in front of her and laughed. "Alright, point taken," she said, still not convinced anyone could truly ruin scrambled eggs.

"This tastes different though," Ethan said, pushing the egg aside with his fork. He glanced up at her.

"What's this?" He stared at the dots of green in his food.

"Parsley. It gives it a nice flavor." At least she hoped it did.

He nodded. "It's good." He went back to shoveling food into his mouth.

"Really good," Patrick added, as though he needed to confirm everything his brother said.

Abigail finished eating then put the coffee-filled mugs on the table. "I thought we could serve the cake with clotted cream today," she suggested gently.

Ethan stared at her, then nodded. "It would be a little bit fancy," he said. "But perhaps we need to be a little bit fancy." He grinned. "You have the best ideas, Abigail."

"I have a lot of ideas," she said quietly, then waved her hands in front of her. "Forget I said anything." She took another mouthful of coffee then jumped up to clear the table.

That look of suspicion crept into his face again. She wasn't sure how long she could keep him at arms length and not tell him the full story, but she was sure it wouldn't be much longer.

She topped up the kettle with water to wash the dishes, then headed out of the kitchen. While she dressed, Ethan entered the bedroom. She pulled her gown up in front of herself.

Her heart pounded – she'd never stood near-naked in front of a man before, even if he was her husband.

He slammed the door shut and stepped over to her. "You do things to me," he whispered while nibbling on her neck.

She shook her head. "We both have work to do. You need to leave the room and let me dress," she said firmly. To her surprise, that's exactly what he did. But not until he pushed his lips to hers.

Abigail decided she liked being married. Especially to Ethan. Except keeping things from him was a huge barrier between them.

She sighed.

Now dressed she strolled out to the kitchen. The dishes had been washed, dried and put away. The kitchen was clean and tidy.

She was at first annoyed that Ethan had infringed on her territory, but understood he was trying to help. No doubt she would find him in the bakery preparing for the day's customers.

Sure enough, he was out there kneading the bread dough.

She busied herself by cleaning the tables, and setting the tables ready for the customers. She would help Ethan by washing the bread tins as they came out of the oven.

Until that could happen, she checked the stocks of the small cakes and slices, and then began to cut the Christmas cake ready for their afternoon rush.

He glanced across at her as she sliced the cake – watched her every move. Had he seen through her charade?

"We need to talk," he told her quietly as he continued kneading the bread.

She looked to the floor. "I know, and I'm sorry," she said in a whisper. "But not now. There's far too much to do before the customers arrive."

He nodded then went back to what he was doing.

Abigail reached for a porcelain bowl then added flour and butter. She began to make breadcrumbs with it, then added the sugar and milk.

He watched curiously but said nothing.

She mixed the ingredients until they formed a dough ball, then sprinkled flour around the counter. "Where is your rolling pin?" She asked the question without blinking an eye, oblivious to the fact he'd be curious about *how* she was doing this more than why she was doing it.

He quirked an eyebrow at her.

"We're nearly out of apple slice," she said blandly, then went back to what she was doing.

His mouth was open, he knew it was, so promptly closed it. "In that drawer," he said, pointing to the large drawer behind her.

She snatched it up and rolled out the pastry, then reached for the apples which she peeled and cut ready for stewing.

When she was done, the apple slice sat in a large tray, waiting to go into the oven. "What else do you want me to make?"

He was too flabbergasted to even think.

"Oh! What about some gingerbread?" She grinned, and he stared at her.

He continued to stare as she cleaned the bowl and began to refill it with the required ingredients. "Do you think that dough has had enough kneading," she said, her voice filled with laughter.

He looked down. She was probably right, but he'd been mesmerized by his wife's baking aptitude.

They really did need to talk, but she was right – now was not the time. Which unfortunately meant it wouldn't happen until tonight.

She stepped over to him and gave him a quick hug. "I'm sorry," she said gently, then stepped away. "I didn't want to hide anything from you." She shrugged her shoulders and went back to her gingerbread mix.

Pulling out the cooked loaves, he wondered what else she was hiding from him. Whatever her secrets, he was convinced they were significant. He stared across at her deft hands preparing the gingerbread.

His father had never bothered with any Christmas fare, and he wondered if it had been his undoing. The bakery had gone downhill for many years under his management, and no matter how much Ethan had tried to help, he had been denied.

The old man had died close to bankruptcy and wouldn't let his sons help. At least Mother wasn't alive to see it.

Abigail pushed the gingerbread mix into a flat tray and sat it aside, again, waiting for an oven to be available.

"Our customers will be very spoiled for choice today," he said, glancing across at her.

She nodded her agreement. "They will. And speaking of customers, it won't be long and they'll be here. I'll make you a sandwich and coffee. You still have time to eat." She brushed her flour covered hands against her apron, then headed toward the kitchen.

Abigail had made his lunch every day since she'd arrived. Normally he had a substantial breakfast then skipped lunch, but she would have none of it.

He liked being looked after by his wife. Just as she seemed to like being looked after by him.

It was a situation where neither of them could lose.

Chapter Eight

"This is delicious, Abigail." Mrs Jensen glanced up at her, wiping her lips with the linen napkin.

She couldn't help but grin. "Thank you, but Ethan is the one who made it."

"He told me it was an old family recipe of yours," the older woman countered. "Where do I sign up to buy a Christmas cake?"

Abigail returned moments later with the order sheet. As she wrote Mrs Jensen's name on the list, she was interrupted.

"Wait!"

Abigail glanced across at her. "You don't want one after all?" She was disappointed, of that she was certain, but it wasn't the end of the world.

Mrs Jensen stared at her, a horrified look on her face. "Good gracious no. Put me down for two," she said. "This would be magnificent to take to the Ladies Auxiliary end of year event." She touched Abigail's arm. "We all take a plate of food, you know."

No, Abigail did not know. But now she did.

"Perhaps next year you will join us," Mrs Jensen said, expectation written all over her face. Instead of committing herself to something she knew nothing about, she spoke to the other women sitting around the table. They each ordered a cake as well. Ethan would be pleased.

As she cleared the plates from each table, more orders were placed. So far a dozen Christmas cakes were ordered. It would be a lot of work, but worth it in the end.

Luckily Christmas was still a matter of weeks away.

Abigail put the list in front of Ethan, who was preparing an order for a customer. He grinned. "You are amazing," he said, leaning in to kiss her cheek.

"It is still early. More orders are likely." She was thrilled. The family recipe that was ingrained in her memory had helped her husband with his business. Luckily he had more than one oven, otherwise it would be a juggling act to have them all finished in time.

Thank you, he mouthed as she returned to the tables and their customers. Her gingerbread and apple slice were both a hit and had nearly sold out by mid-afternoon.

Ethan said her apple slice was far better than his, which filled her heart with warmth.

As the sun began to set, she became nervous. It was nearly time to close the bakery. She promised Ethan they would talk tonight.

Not that she wanted to discuss her personal life in front of Patrick, but while he remained, she had little choice.

He'd been working on the bakery cupboards and shelves again today, and announced he was finally done. Soon he would leave.

As much as she liked Patrick, his departure meant she would finally be alone with her new husband. She hoped it would bring them closer.

She removed the table cloths for washing and scrubbed the tables, as was her habit at the end of each day.

Abigail looked up to see Ethan staring at her. Was he thinking about their discussion tonight? Or was something else on his mind?

He wandered over to where she worked, and put his arms around her. "You never cease to amaze me," he said, pulling her closer.

It was difficult to continue scrubbing with her husband holding her tight, so Abigail stood. He turned her around in his arms and kissed her forehead.

"I know it's difficult to talk with Patrick here, so why don't we go for a stroll? Just the two of us."

She stared into his eyes. He really was trying to make it easier for her. "Let me check on the stew first, then we can go."

She finished cleaning then pulled off her apron and headed for the kitchen. Abigail stirred the stew and breathed in the aromatic fragrance of it. She'd always loved the smells of food cooking, and that was probably her undoing. Her mother had baked for as far back as Abigail could remember.

The house always felt like home because of it.

After her mother had died, Abigail missed that feeling so much, she began to bake in her spare time. It was both a joy and a regret.

Realizing she was as good a cook as her mother, Father had roped her in to work in the bakery from a very young age.

By the time she was fourteen, she spent more of her time in the bakery than anywhere else. She'd become the equivalent of a slave by the time she'd fled her father's arranged marriage.

Abigail washed her hands with thoughts of days gone by invading her memory. She tried to shake them away but they refused to budge.

She took a deep cleansing breath and slowly let it out again. She already felt better.

"Ready?" Ethan entered the kitchen carrying a loaf of leftover bread. He informed his brother of their intentions and headed for the front door.

They snatched up their coats on the way. It was already chilly outside, and the closer to Christmas it got, the colder it would be.

With only two weeks before Christmas snow would be falling very soon.

They each pulled on their gloves and wrapped a scarf around their necks. Abigail braced herself for the cold chill she knew would hit her face as they left the warm and toasty house.

"Where are we going?"

Ethan shrugged his shoulders. "Nowhere in particular. I thought it would be good to get out of the house."

"Away from your brother, do you mean?" She gave him a tentative smile.

"That too." He reached for her hand, and it comforted her. "To be honest, I'll miss him, but it will be nice to be only the two of us." He glanced across at her. "We don't even know each other. Not really."

"I know that you are a kind and gentle person," she said quietly.

"And I know you can cook far better than any home cook." He stared at her, then squeezed her hand.

They walked along Main Street in silence, until they reached a wooden bench outside the butcher shop. It had already closed for the day, so they were assured of privacy.

"Maybe start at the beginning," he said gently, nudging her toward opening up, but not being aggressive.

"My father is a baker." The words were out much quicker than she'd anticipated. She felt so much better for having said them.

She glanced up at him, to find Ethan frowning. "And you chose to marry me, another baker." He looked thoroughly confused.

She shook her head vigorously. "No, I didn't." She explained how she'd opened the letter as the train pulled into Dayton Falls.

Sadness overtook him. "If you want an annulment…"

"No!" She grabbed his hand. "No, I don't. My father is a bully and a scoundrel. I'm almost certain he gambled me away, perhaps even the bakery."

He stared at her, shock written all over his face. They sat in silence until finally he asked her to explain.

She told him about Peter Jones, and her father contracting their marriage into the sale of the bakery. About how badly Mr Jones had treated her during earlier encounters, and how she had to flee or be married off to that obnoxious man.

He might have only been a few years older than her, but Abigail couldn't abide the man and so had fled.

When she looked down, his hands were shaking. She glanced up at him and his face was red. "You're angry with me – I can't say I blame you."

He reached out and held both her hands. "I didn't want to become a slave to another baker, so I hid my past." She glanced up into his face. "I'm really sorry," she said, touching his cheek ever so gently.

"I'm not angry with you," he said firmly. "I am furious with your father and this…Peter Jones. How dare they treat you so badly?"

He leaned in and pulled her into a hug. Abigail suddenly felt safe, and wanted.

Her eyes filled with tears, and she did what she should have done a long time ago. She cried.

Ethan patted her back, and rubbed his hands across her back. "I'm sorry you had to endure that," he whispered. "I promise to always appreciate you. We're partners in the bakery – I will never make a slave of you."

She pulled back and stared at him. "Really?"

"I promise."

She wiped the tears from her eyes. "I don't mind helping in the bakery. In fact, I enjoy it, just not to the extent my father forced me to do." She gave him a tentative smile and leaned into him again.

"Oh, I almost forgot," he said, reaching into his pocket. "This arrived today." He pulled out a tiny box and opened it, then place the shiny gold wedding ring on her finger.

"This is for you, Mrs Harper."

She stared down at the plain gold ring on her left hand. It was the best gift she'd ever received.

* * *

It was a bitter-sweet day. Patrick was leaving for Great Falls today.

There was a promise of a great future for him there. With the town expanding at a rapid rate, there would be months of work for him. Perhaps even years.

It was what he'd dreamed of most of his adult life. Ethan leaned in and hugged his brother tight.

"Thanks for everything, Patrick. Keep in touch, let me know how it's all going."

His brother held him tight as though he'd never let go. Suddenly he dropped his arms and turned to Abigail, hugging her tightly.

She looked over her shoulder at Ethan. "That's my wife you're hugging."

Patrick stared at his brother. "Why do you think I'm hugging her for so long?" He laughed at his own words. Ethan couldn't help but join in.

"All aboard!" The conductor put out one last call.

He watched as Patrick boarded the train. He felt like a part of him had left. Abigail leaned in close, and he put his arms around her. "It feels like I've lost a big part of my life," he said quietly.

"I know," she whispered. "But there's a whole new adventure ahead of you."

He turned to her and smiled. "You're right." The train pulled out with a jerk, and they turned to leave.

Ethan looked back over his shoulder and spotted his brother waving goodbye. It really was the end of an era for him.

When they arrived back at the bakery, there was already a queue of people waiting. He'd put up a sign the bakery would be opened late today due to Patrick's departure.

They'd become an integral part of the town, so people were happy to wait. He and Abigail had got up earlier today to ensure there were plenty of supplies for the day's customers.

The moment they walked inside, the havoc began all over again.

* * *

Almost two weeks had passed since Patrick had left. Ethan had received a telegraph to say he'd arrived okay and had found lodgings – with meals included.

Abigail had laughed about that. Patrick loved his food, there was no doubt about it.

"Since it's nearly Christmas, I thought we should get a Christmas tree for the bakery."

Ethan glanced up as Abigail sipped her morning coffee. "That sounds nice. Is that what your father did?"

She laughed. "Heavens no. If it took any effort, it didn't happen." She took another sip. "I just thought it would be nice. Dayton Falls is a lovely little town, and most of the other businesses have decorated their stores already."

She was right. The Mercantile decorated a couple of weeks back, and the shoe store put their decorations up last week.

"Alright." He pulled out his pocket-watch. "Let's go now and find a tree."

She stared at him as though he'd grown horns. "Are you kidding? We have to bake bread."

He stood and glanced down at her. "We never sell bread until mid-afternoon. Just this once, let's break our routine."

He was feeling joyful today. He didn't know what it was, but his heart was filled with love.

The moment Abigail was ready, they rugged up and left the house. It felt strange to not be in the bakery preparing bread for the day. Ethan knew his father would be admonishing him if he was here, but he needed to do this. For Abigail.

They headed toward the livery and hired a wagon then headed to the small forest outside of town.

They soon came across a stand of suitable trees. "This one?" Ethan said, standing next to a fine looking tree.

Abigail looked pensive. She stepped toward the worst looking tree of all. "This one," she said, sorrow in her voice. "This tree is unloved. We need to nurture it."

He laughed, but she wasn't laughing.

"I know what it feels like to be unloved," she said quietly. "And I think you do too. We can add some decorations to it, and make it the best tree around."

"Alright," Ethan said, against his better judgement. He got the saw from the wagon and cut down the spindly tree Abigail had chosen. "I still think that other one was better."

"You didn't return me for something better, did you?"

He studied her for a few moments. She was right. His wife was far from perfect when she arrived. She was fragile and uncertain, but look at her now. She was perfect. Beyond perfect.

He placed the tree on the wagon then reached out and put his arms around her. "You are something else," he said gently. "Is it any wonder I love you so much."

The words were out before he could stop them. He'd loved her almost from the first moment they'd met. There was something about Abigail that caught his attention. Perhaps it was her forthrightness, or maybe it was her beauty.

He couldn't be certain, but he knew from the moment he set eyes on her, she was the one. His forever love.

"Oh Ethan," she wailed. "Do you really mean that?" She rested her head on his shoulders. "I didn't think anyone could ever love me. Except for my mother."

She wrapped her arms around him and held him tight. "I love you too," she whispered. "You are such a kind and gentle person, and you treat me like an equal. I can't believe my luck with finding you."

He lifted his head and kissed her lips, gently at first, but then more urgently. "I think it's time to get home," he said when he finally came up for air.

He winked at her, and Abigail wondered when he thought he was going to bake bread today.

Epilogue

One year later...

Abigail squatted down at the bakery Christmas tree decorating it. Ethan was kneading bread and watched as his wife did what she loved to do – make the season more festive.

"No, no, no!" She screamed and tried to stand. "This can't be happening."

Ethan rushed to her side and helped her to stand, then looked to the floor. Her waters had broken. The baby wasn't due for another couple of weeks, but babies were unpredictable.

At least that's what Doc Grogan had told him.

He lifted her gently and carried Abigail into the bedroom, laying her on the bed. "I'll go get the doc," he said. "Don't you move."

She nodded but knowing her stubbornness, he wouldn't count on it. "Towels, grab some towels," she shouted urgently as he was about to leave to get the doc.

He did as he was told and slid them under her.

His heart was pounding – he was going to be a dad. Okay, so he knew that for the past six months or more, but it was more eminent now.

He ran in a circle. What was he doing?

"Get the doc," Abigail shouted. She knew him far too well.

"Getting the doc," he said, sticking his head through the doorway.

"Go! Or you might have to deliver this baby." His eyes opened in shock. Was she serious?

He turned around and ran. "Going," he called as he left the house.

Doc Grogan lived in town, so he didn't have far to go. He ran as fast as his feet could take him.

"You seem in a hurry," Mrs Jensen said as he ran past.

"Baby's coming," he shouted as he continued on his way.

"Oh my goodness," she said, and began hurrying toward the house. Mrs Jensen would be a big help, and was good friends with Abigail, so he didn't try to stop her.

It seemed like forever later when he rejoined his wife, Mrs Jensen by her side.

"Be a dear and put on the kettle. And some pans of water – as much as you can."

He leaned into his wife, and patted her hand. "Everything will be alright. Doc's on his way." He kissed her gently on the lips.

She looked up at him. "This is all your fault," she said between gritted teeth.

He laughed.

"I would leave about now, if I were you," the doc said behind him. "Childbirth seems to bring out the worst."

"I'll put the water on," he said, backing out of the room.

Bertha Grogan, the doc's wife, arrived around the same time. She shoo'd him out of the house. He did what he knew Abigail would want him to do – he made bread.

Despite having closed the adjoining door so he couldn't hear her screams, the sounds were only slightly muffled. It killed him that he wasn't there to support her.

Instead of kneading the bread, he pounded it. Ethan was certain it would be the worst bread he'd ever made. But he honestly didn't care.

But Abigail would.

He threw the dough into the rubbish and started over. He kneaded the dough with love, as he normally would, and placed it in the tins, then the oven. Thankfully it was the last batch for the day.

He needed to start on the muffins next. Despite the closeness to Christmas Day, they would be busy. In fact it was busier because of the celebrations. People were stocking up before the holidays.

Thanks to Abigail, the bakery was thriving. Thanks to her also, he was happier than he'd ever been.

The adjoining door flew open after what seemed like hours. "Congratulations Dad. Come and meet your son."

Mrs Grogan leaned in and hugged him and Ethan had to fight back tears. He was a father. "What about Abigail? Is she alright?"

"She's fine. Come and see for yourself."

He almost ran toward the bedroom, then stood in the doorway staring at the scene before him. His beautiful wife sat up supported by pillows behind her, holding their newborn baby boy.

He had streaks of red hair just like his mother.

"Come and say hello to your son." Abigail looked pale, and she sounded tired, but he could see she was filled with joy.

He sat on the edge of the bed and hugged them both. "Thank you," he whispered as he brushed the tears from his eyes.

"That makes two of the best Christmas gifts I've ever had." She stared at him in confusion. "You and our baby boy."

He leaned in and kissed her forehead. "I love you Abigail Harper, more than words can ever say."

As he pulled back he saw the trickle of tears run down her face. "I love you too," she said quietly. And in that moment, Ethan knew they would have a long and happy life together.

Scroll down for Abigail's Christmas Cake Recipe

From the Author

Thank you so much for reading my book – I hope you enjoyed it.

I would greatly appreciate you leaving a review where you purchased, even if it is only a one-liner. It helps to have my books more visible!

This was the last book in this series. If you would like to read Patrick's story, check out the spin-off series, Brides of Montana.

Emily is the first book in that series, and you can read Patrick and Emily's story in that book.

About the

Author

Multi-published, award-winning and bestselling author Cheryl Wright, former secretary, debt collector, account manager, writing coach, and shopping tour hostess, loves reading.

She writes both historical and contemporary western romance, as well as romantic suspense.

She lives in Melbourne, Australia, and is married with two adult children and has six grandchildren. When she's not writing, she can be found in her craft room making greeting cards.

Website: *http://www.cheryl-wright.com/*

Facebook Reader Group:
https://www.facebook.com/groups/cherylwrightaut hor/

Join My Newsletter:

https://cheryl-wright.com/newsletter/
(and receive a free book)

Christmas Cake Recipe

This Christmas cake recipe has been in my husband's family for generations and has been adjusted along the way. His mother gave it to me after we were married in January 1975, and I've been using it ever since.

It's a really moist cake, and has also been used for wedding cakes.

*It is important to note this cake does not rise a lot.

Into a large basin or mixing bowl place the following mixture:

1 kilogram (or 2 lb) mixed fruit

2 cups (1 lb) brown sugar

2 tablespoons each Sherry and Orange juice, or if preferred, 4 tablespoons of either. (You may need more to ensure all ingredients are wet – I've been known to double this amount.)

Stir well and soak overnight, covered in plastic wrap to prevent mixture drying out.

If unable to soak overnight, soak for minimum of two hours

Next day, stir to separate any ingredients that have melded together overnight. There is no problem if they are stuck, it's just easier to mix if you separate the ingredients at this point.

Now add 1/2 teaspoon each of the following spices:

Nutmeg, ginger, cinnamon, salt, and bicarbonate soda.

Mix until all ingredients are combined.

Add 2 oz (60 grams) chopped almonds. Mix well.

Combine 250g (1/2 lb) butter and 1/2 cup (4 oz) milk. Heat in saucepan over slow heat only until butter is melted. Do not allow to boil.

Add butter/milk mixture to fruit etc, then add:

3 beaten eggs

1/2 teaspoon vanilla essence

1/2 teaspoon lemon essence

Now slowly add 3 cups plain flour, mixing between each addition. Blend in well and pour into a paper lined tin.

(I use 9 inch or 23 cm wide tin, with height of 2 1/2 inch or 6 cm. this is a perfect fit for the mixture)

Bake 275 degrees F (140 degrees C) for approx 5 1/2 to 6 hours. (May take less time in fan-forced oven – anything from 4 1/2 to 5 hours) Cooks best if piece of brown paper is placed loosely over top of cake. *If you use a different size tin, cooking time will need to be adjusted.

Do not open oven door for at least 2 1/2 hours.